PJMASKS

THE FLYING FACTORY!

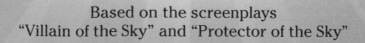

Based on the screenplays
"Villain of the Sky" and "Protector of the Sky"

Ready-to-Read

Simon Spotlight
New York London Toronto Sydney New Delhi

SIMON SPOTLIGHT
An imprint of Simon & Schuster Children's Publishing Division
1230 Avenue of the Americas, New York, New York 10020
This Simon Spotlight edition July 2020
Adapted by May Nakamura from the series PJ Masks
All rights reserved, including the right of reproduction in whole or in part in any form.
SIMON SPOTLIGHT, READY-TO-READ, and colophon are registered trademarks of Simon & Schuster, Inc.
For information about special discounts for bulk purchases, please contact Simon & Schuster Special Sales at 1-866-506-1949 or business@simonandschuster.com.
Manufactured in the United States of America 0520 LAK
10 9 8 7 6 5 4 3 2 1
ISBN 978-1-5344-6430-8 (hc)
ISBN 978-1-5344-6429-2 (pbk)
ISBN 978-1-5344-6431-5 (eBook)

Greg, Amaya, and Connor
are walking in the city.

A metal streetlamp
is missing.
They know Romeo must
be up to no good!

Connor
becomes
Catboy!

Greg
becomes
Gekko!

Amaya
becomes
Owlette!

They are the PJ Masks!

Owlette uses her
Owl Eyes to look for
the metal parts.

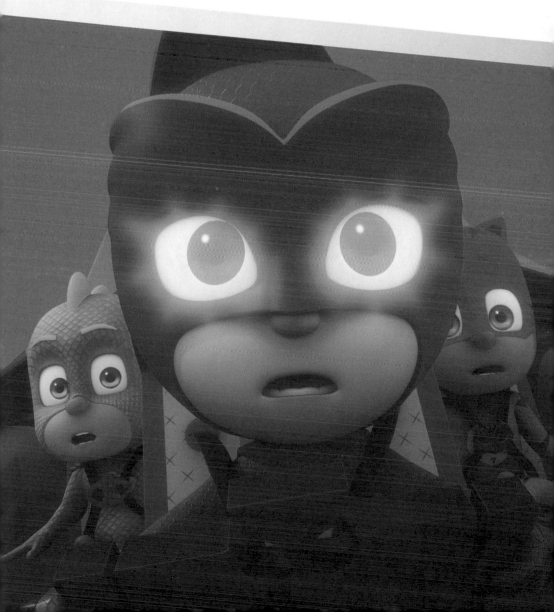

Owlette spots

a big factory

in the forest.

Its tube sucks in
streetlamps
and other metal things.

Romeo appears

from inside the factory.

What is his plan?

Many robots
guard the factory.
They look just like
PJ Robot!

Owlette has an idea.

PJ Robot can dress up
and spy on Romeo!

PJ Robot

enters the factory.

He sees

a large control room.

Then Romeo tests
all his robots.

PJ Robot gets caught!

The factory begins
to shake.
It lifts off the ground
and into the sky!

"Leaping lizards!"

Gekko says.

"That is a flying factory!"

"It is getting away!"

Catboy yells.

Romeo is using the metal parts from the city for his Flying Factory.

The factory is releasing
big clouds of gunk!

They spread
all over the city.

"I will not take the clouds
away until everyone
obeys me forever!"
Romeo says.

"It is time to be a hero!"

Owlette shouts.

Owlette saves PJ Robot.

Gekko distracts Romeo
and his robots.

Owlette changes
the controls.

The tube starts to whir.

It sucks in all the clouds.

The sky is clear again!

The PJ Masks have
defeated Romeo and
his Flying Factory!

PJ Masks all shout hooray!

Because in the night,

they saved the day . . .

and the sky!